THE BLUE LOTUS
藍蓮花

TINTIN AND SNOWY are in India, guests of the Maharaja of Gaipajama, enjoying a well-earned rest. The evil gang of international drug-smugglers, encountered in *Cigars of the Pharaoh*, has been smashed and its members are behind bars. With one exception. Only the mysterious gang-leader is unaccounted for: he disappeared over a cliff.

But questions have still to be answered. What of the terrible Rajaijah juice, the 'poison of madness'? Where were the shipments of opium going, hidden in the false cigars? And who really was the master-mind behind the operation?

How can a dog get a wink of sleep? Not a minute's peace since he fell for short-wave radio!...

There it is again. That's the station I've been trying to identify...

It doesn't make any sense... What can it possibly mean?

RRCQ 15.30 direct special attention charles yokohama urgently going oddly slow istanbul ten nasty gaps in saturday means tibetan medicine easily changes west ekombi

It must have some meaning... but what?

My direction-finder shows WSW, ENE. In theory the transmitter should be along a line in the same direction, passing through Gaipajama.

Tintin Sahib, the Maharaja requests your presence.

Thank you. I'll come.

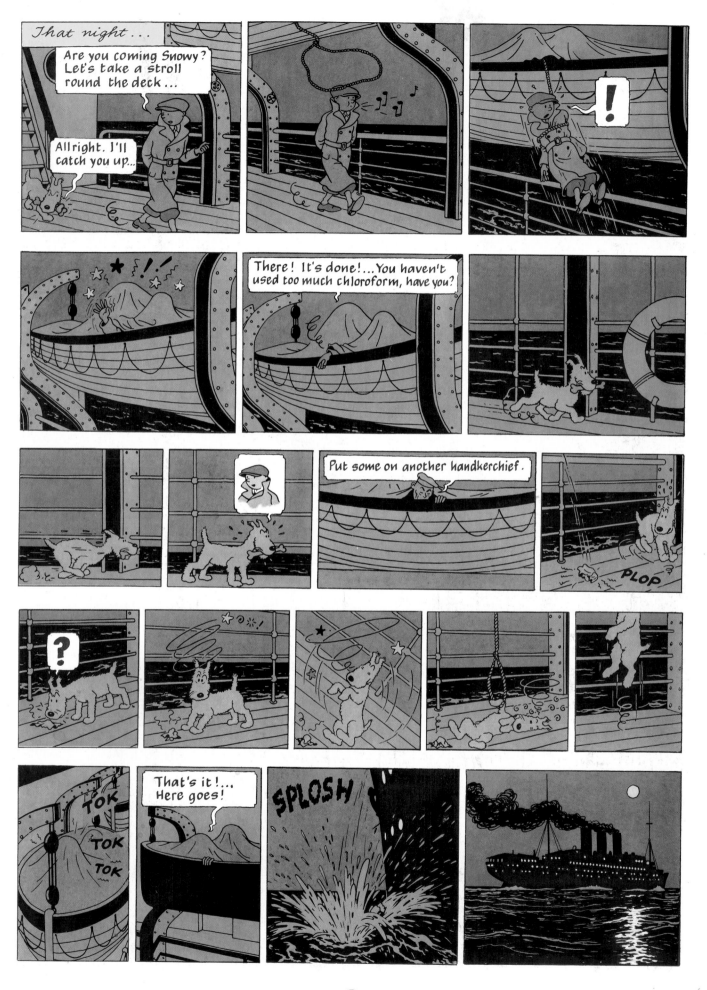

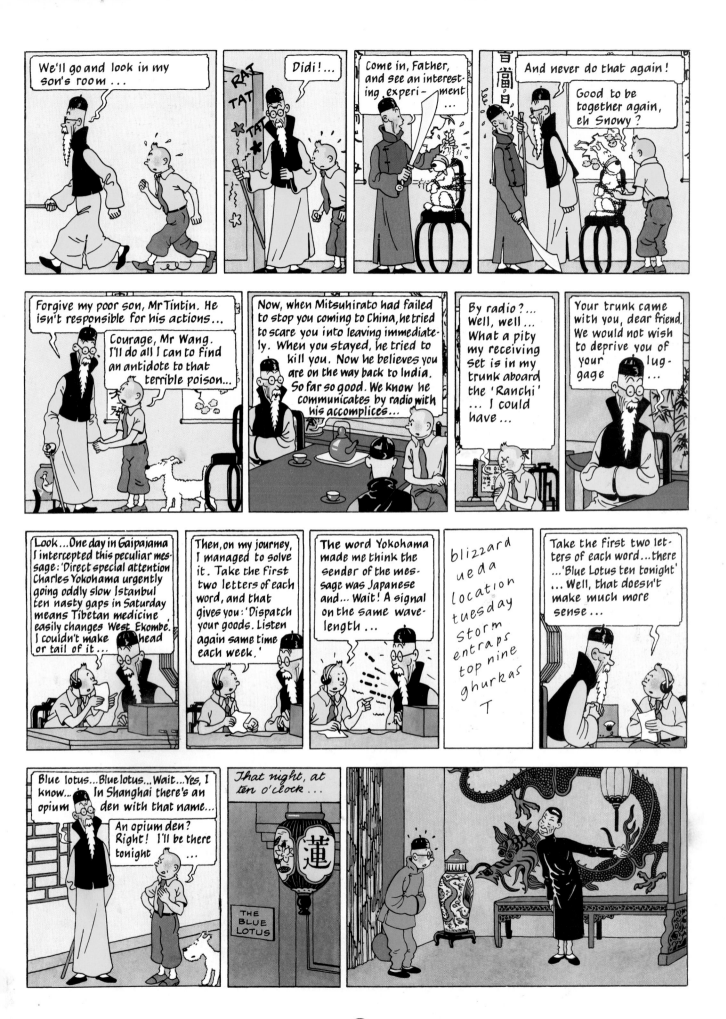

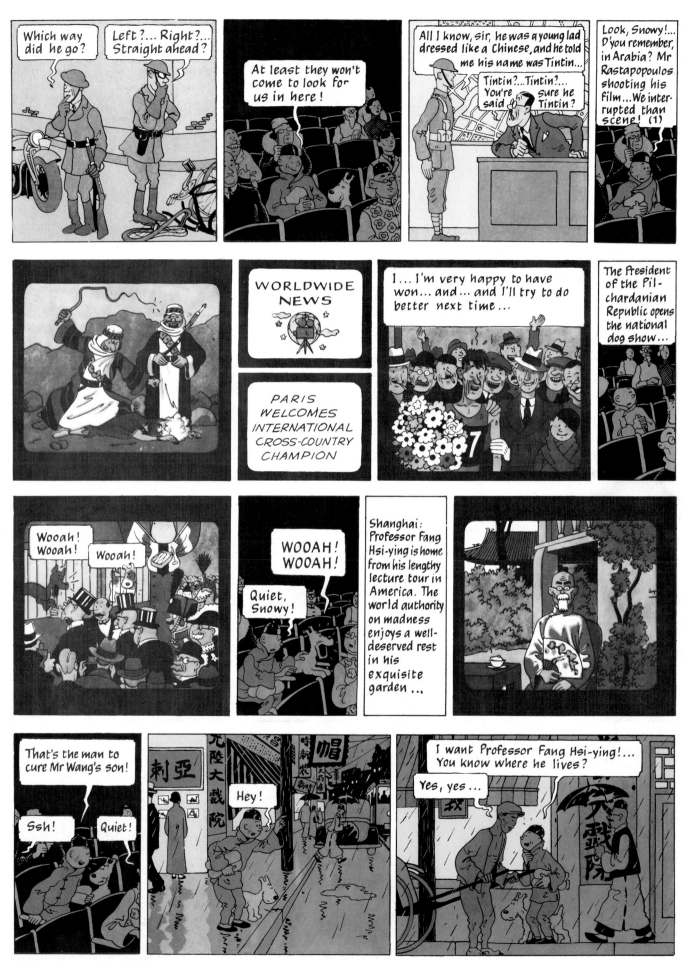

(1) See *Cigars of the Pharaoh*

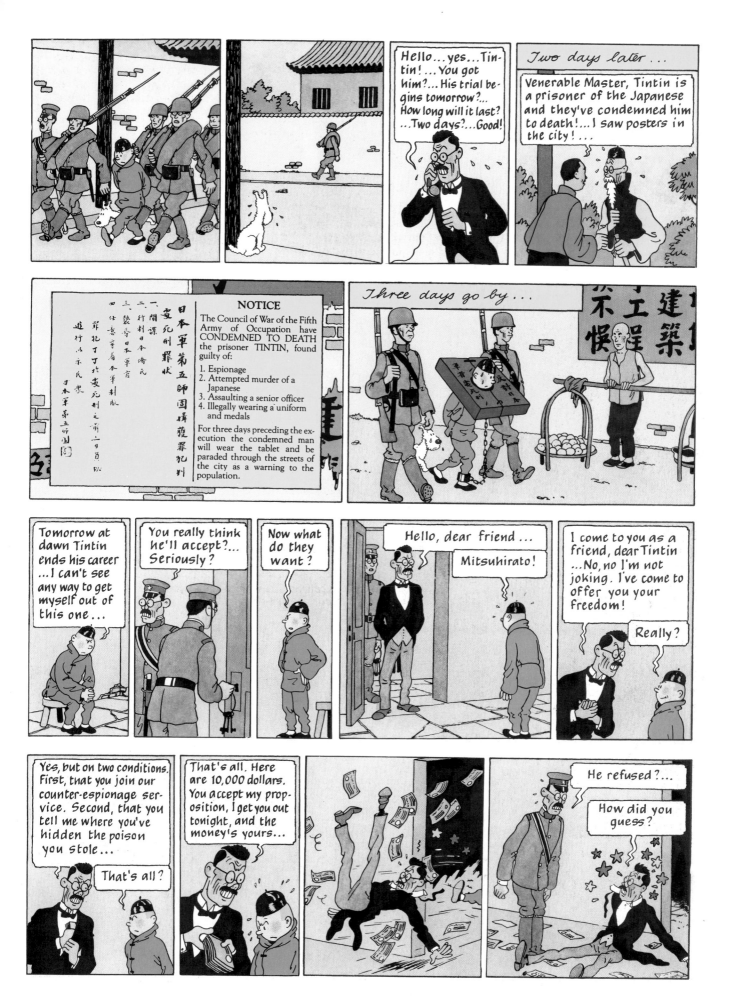

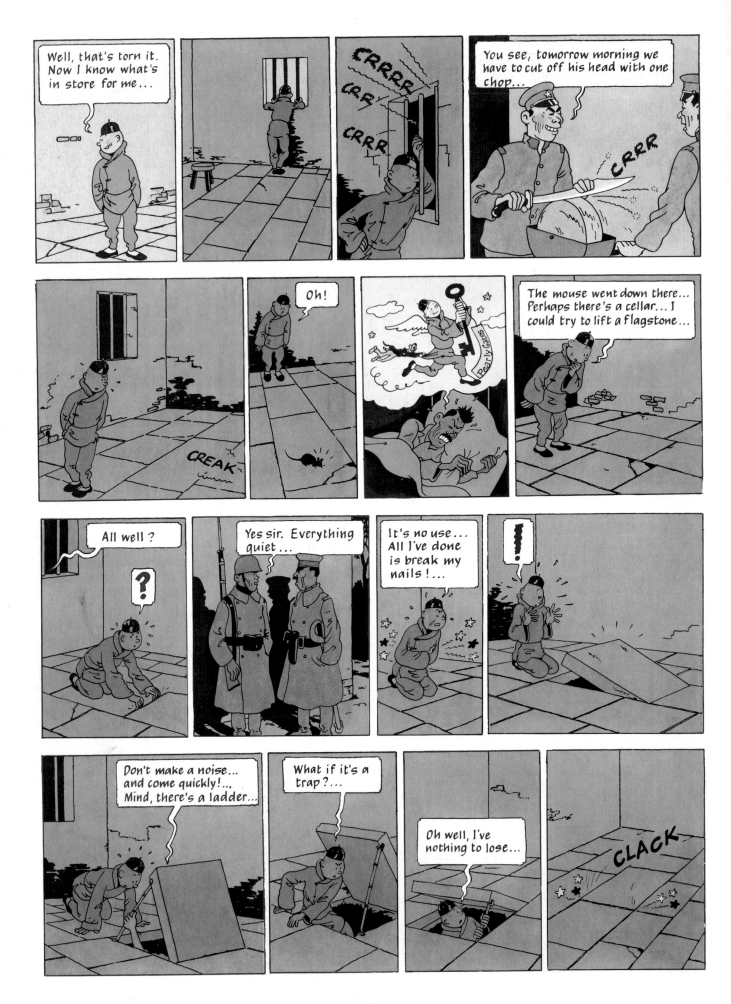

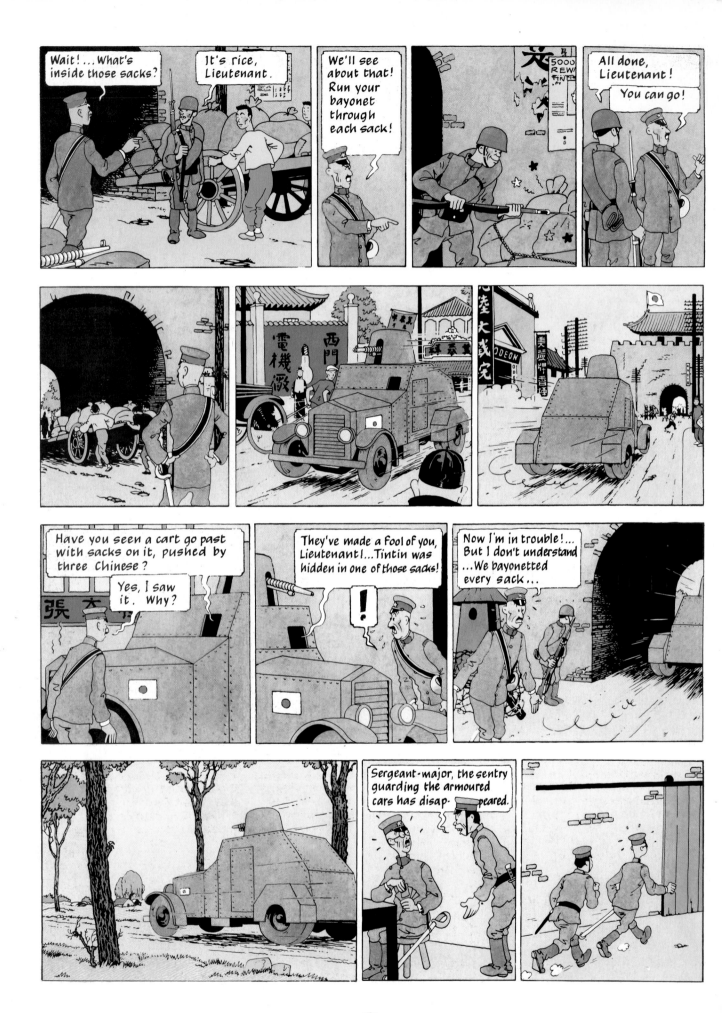

Panel 1: What an excellent idea!... It remains to be seen if the Chief of Police will agree...

Oh, I can vouch for him, General... Look...

Panel 2: 9, J. M. Dawson, Chief of Police of the International Settlement, owe the sum of 10,700 dollars to Mr Mitsuhirato

J. M. Dawson

Shanghai 18. X. 31

He! he! Marvellous!

Panel 3: Next day...

Mr Mitsuhirato? ... Very well, show him in...

Panel 4: Good morning, Mr Mitsuhirato. What fair wind blows you here?

Panel 5: I come to beg a favour... If you agree to grant it, then in return I'll forget all about that trifling sum of money you owe me...

What are you getting at?

Panel 6: Quite simply...Tintin is now in Hukow... And I want you to get him arrested...

Hukow?...That's Chinese territory. My jurisdiction is limited to the International Settlement...

Panel 7: Of course, but the Chinese wouldn't refuse you permission to go after a European, even outside the Settlement...

Panel 8: No, maybe not... But what reason can I give?... Tintin hasn't committed any crime...

Panel 9: A reason?... How should I know? ... What if you suspect him of involvement in the kidnapping of Professor Fang Hsi-ying, for example...

That's an idea...

Panel 10: Chinese Police Headquarters... Good morning, Mr Dawson ...What?...Fang Hsi-ying?...You've got a lead?...A European? And you want a pass for your detectives... Of course...

Panel 11: That's it...We'll have the pass tomorrow morning. My men will leave as soon as it comes.

Panel 12: A happy arrangement. You arrest Tintin, and let him go for lack of evidence ...By chance, he falls into our hands...

Right... and you cancel that trifling debt of mine...

Panel 13: Hukow...

Panel 14: *(no text)*

Panel 15: My father had a friend in the town...We'll ask if we can stay with him...

44

46

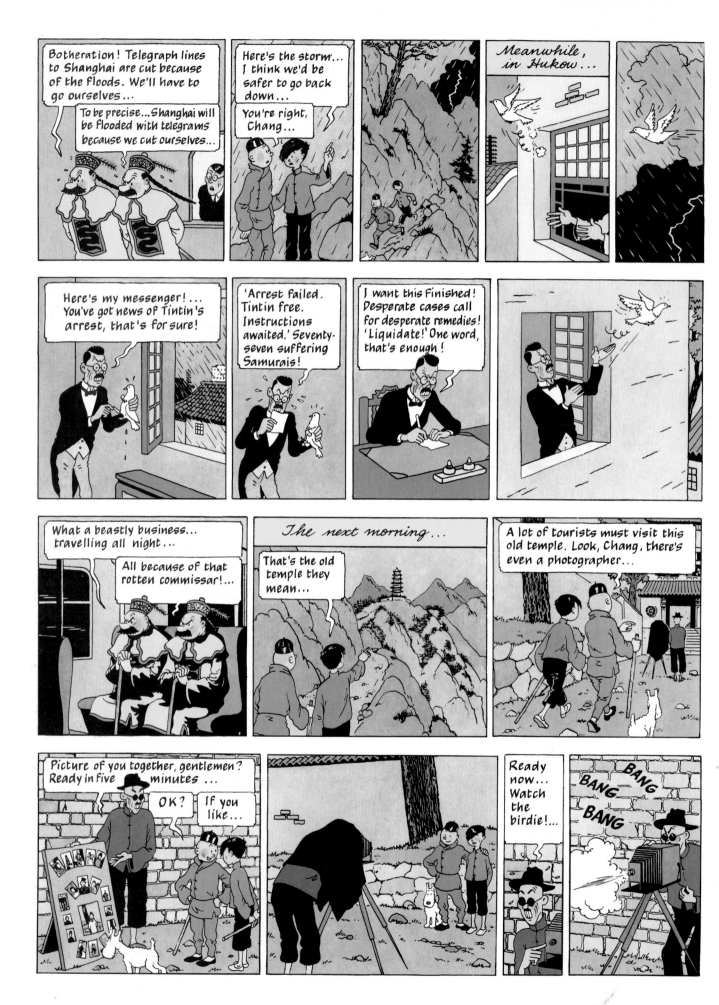

(1) See *Cigars of the Pharaoh*

SHANGHAI NEWS

上海報

FANG HSI-YING FOUND: Professor Prisoner in Opium Den

SHANGHAI, Wednesday: Professor Fang Hsi-ying has been found! The good news was flashed to us this morning.

Last week eminent scholar Fang disappeared on his way home from a party given by a friend. Police efforts to trace him were unavailing. No clues were found.

Young European reporter Tintin joined in the hunt for the missing man of science. Earlier we reported incidents involving Tintin and the occupying Japanese forces. Secret society Sons of the Dragon aided Tintin in the rescue. Fang Hsi-ying was kidnapped by an international gang of drug smugglers, now all safely in police custody.

Professor Fang Hsi-ying pictured just after his release.

A wireless transmitter was found by police at Blue Lotus opium den. The transmitter was used by the drug smugglers to communicate with their ships on the high seas. Information radioed included sea routes, ports to be avoided, points of embarkation and unloading.

Home of Japanese subject Mitsuhirato was also searched. No comment, say police on reports of seizure of top-secret documents. Unconfirmed rumours suggest the papers concern undercover political acitivity by a neighbouring power. Speculation mounts that they disclose recent Shanghai-Nanking railway incident as a pretext for extended Japanese occupation. League of Nations officials in Geneva will study the captured documents.

———

TINTIN'S OWN STORY

This morning, hero of the hour Mr Tintin, talked to us about his adventures.

Tintin, rescuer of Professor Fang Hsi-ying, with Snowy, his faithful companion.

The young reporter is the guest of Mr Wang Chen-yee at his host's picturesque villa on the Nanking road. When we called, our hero, young and smiling, greeted us wearing Chinese dress. Could this really be the scourge of the terrible Shanghai gangsters?

After our greetings and congratulations, we asked Mr Tintin to tell us how he succeeded in smashing the most dangerous organisation.

Mr Wang, a tall, elderly, venerable man with an impish smile said:

"You must tell the world it is entirely due to him that my wife, my son and I are alive today!"

With these words our interview was concluded, and we said farewell to the friendly reporter and his kindly host.

L.G.T.

Young people carry posters of Tintin through Shanghai streets.

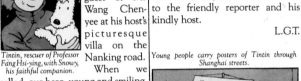